This book belongs to:

_____

Note to parents and carers

Many children are now taught to read using the phonic approach. This means they are taught to look at the letters, say the sounds, and then blend them to make a word. So, for example, children blend **c/a/t** to make the word **cat**, and **sh/o/p** to make **shop**.

When children have completed their initial phonics learning, they are ready to apply it to reading real books. Ladybird's **Superhero Phonic Readers** are planned for this exciting stage.

Some words are hard to read using beginner phonics. These words are often known as 'tricky words'. Some of these occur frequently in the English language so it is useful for children to memorize them.

Have fun doing our Tricky Words Memory Quiz on page 30. This features the most useful tricky words from the story.

How to use Superhero Phonic Readers:

☆ Start at level one and gradually progress through the series. Each story is a little bit longer than the last and uses more grown-up vocabulary.

☆ Children will be able to read **Superhero Phonic Readers** for themselves. Let your child read to you, and share the excitement!

☆ If your child finds any words difficult, help him or her to work out the sounds in the word.

☆ Early readers can be concentrating so hard on the words that they sometimes don't fully grasp the overall meaning of what they read. The puzzle questions on pages 28 and 29 will help with this. Have fun talking about them together.

☆ There is a reward chart at the back of the book - young readers can fill this in and stick it on the wall.

☆ The Ladybird website **www.ladybird.com** features a wealth of information about phonics and reading.

☆ Enjoy reading together!

Geraldine Taylor
Ladybird Educational Consultant

Educational Consultant: Geraldine Taylor

Phonics Consultant: Marj Newbury

A catalogue record for this book is available from the British Library

Published by Ladybird Books Ltd
80 Strand, London, WC2R 0RL
A Penguin Company

2 4 6 8 10 9 7 5 3 1
© LADYBIRD BOOKS LTD MMIX. This edition MMX
LADYBIRD and the device of a Ladybird are trademarks of Ladybird Books Ltd

ISBN: 978-1-40930-784-6

Printed in China

Superhero Phonic Readers

The Super Twins

written by Dick Crossley

illustrated by Deborah van de Leijgraaf

Meet Max Chan and his sister, Min.
As you can see, Max and Min are twins.
Now, all twins are special. But Max and Min are
extra-special. They both have a fantastic power.

Max and Min can change size when they rub their tummies. Min can shrink.

And as Min gets smaller,
and smaller,
and smaller...

…Max gets bigger,
and bigger,
and bigger!

The twins can change back to their normal size
whenever they want, by rubbing their tummies again.

Max and Min found out about their powers when they were babies.

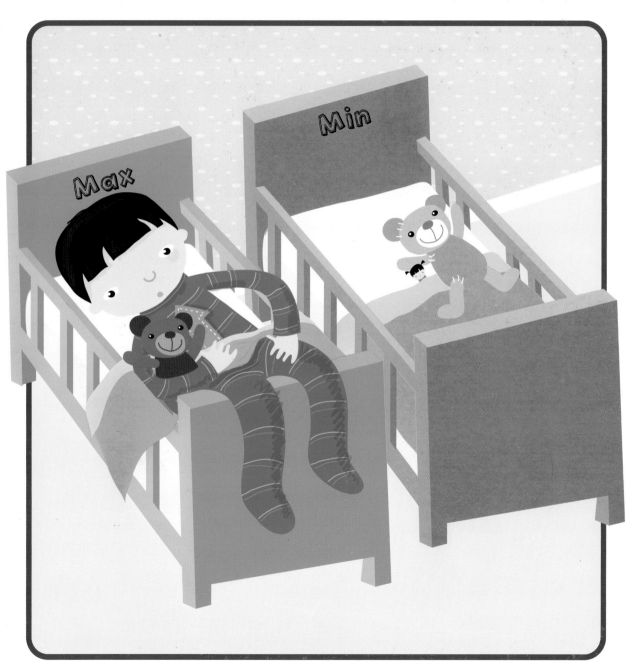

The twins' powers came in very handy at school.
They had fun getting smaller and bigger.

Then, when the twins were ten years old, they used their powers to rescue a man. He was trapped in a crane, high up in the sky.

So Max got much bigger and Min got much smaller.

The lock on the crane door had broken.
Max lifted Min up and put her inside the lock.
Min went to work. In seconds, she had picked the lock.

The man got out of the crane and stepped onto Max. He slid down Max's back and was soon safe on the ground.

The rescue story was on the news.
Max and Min were superheroes.

From then on, lots of people asked for their help.
When Big Ben stopped ticking, Max was just the
right size to lend a hand.

When the Queen's tooth needed filling, Min helped out.
She was a perfect little dentist.

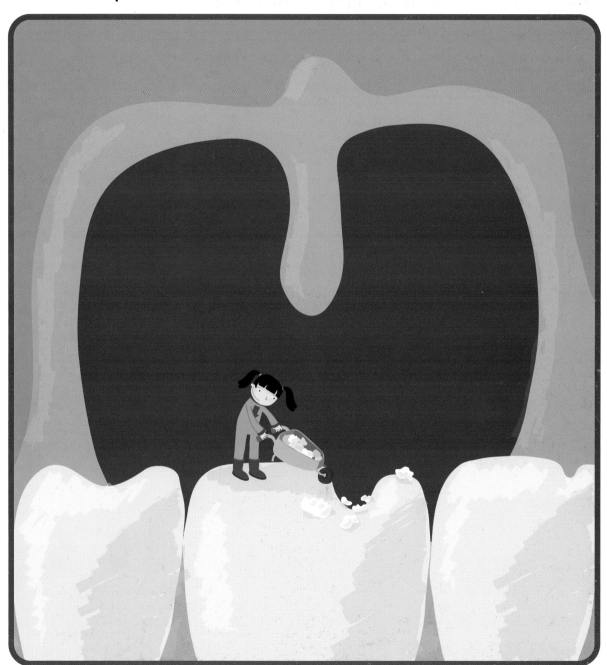

And at Christmas time, both twins helped with the big tree in London. Soon, everyone found out about the twins' powers.

People in other parts of the world started to ask for their help. When the Statue of Liberty dropped her torch, the American President rang the twins…

…so that Max could hand it back.

When the Princess of Spain got nits, she sent a letter to the twins…

…so that Min could hunt them down.

And when the keepers at Taronga Zoo got chicken pox, the Australian Prime Minister made a call…

…to ask the twins to look after the animals.

The twins were asked to take on harder and harder tasks.
"Could Max help to change a light bulb…?"

"Would Min fix the electronics on this rocket?"

"Could Max sort out the Leaning Tower in Italy…?"

"Would the twins lend a hand with a spot of cleaning…?"

But however hard the job might seem,
Max and Min were up to it.

Today, Max and Min are world-famous.

Their special helpline never stops ringing.

They use their powers to help people all round the globe.
From Africa…

...to Antarctica.

So, if you ever need help, no matter what the problem is, you know who to call…

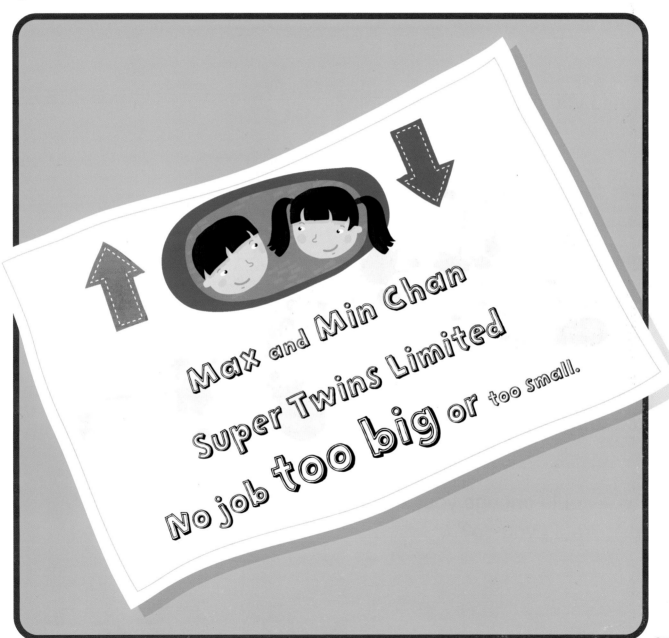

Max and Min Chan
Super Twins Limited
No job too big or too small.

Superhero Secret Puzzles

⭐ What is extra-special about Max and Min?

⭐ Would you rather be Max or Min?

⭐ How does the man get out of the crane?

⭐ What job does Min do for the Queen?

⭐ Why did Max and Min help out at Taronga Zoo?

⭐ What famous places can you find in the story?

⭐ If you could change your size,
what would you do?

Look at these pictures from the story and say the order they should go in.

A

B

C

D

Answer on page 30.

Tricky Words Memory Quiz

Can you remember these words from the story?

See if you can read them super-fast.

you	out	people
are	were	her
all	school	could
they	he	asked
have	was	would
when	me	round
their	I	no
the	so	what
to	work	know
want	she	who

What else can you remember?

Can you put the book down and say what happens in the story?

The answer to the picture puzzle on page 29 is: A, D, C, B.

Ask an adult to cut this page out for you. You can stick it on your wall.

I'm a phonic
Superhero

I can read all of **The Super Twins**.

I can read all the tricky words.

By _____

Date _____

level
7